# LEGO STAR WARS

## THE EMPIRE STRIKES OUT

**BY ACE LANDERS**
**BASED ON THE SCREENPLAY BY MICHAEL PRICE**

SCHOLASTIC INC.

Scholastic Children's Books,
Euston House, 24 Eversholt Street,
London NW1 1DB, UK

A division of Scholastic Ltd
London ~ New York ~ Toronto ~ Sydney ~ Auckland
Mexico City ~ New Delhi ~ Hong Kong

This book was first published in the US in 2013 by Scholastic Inc.

Published in the UK by Scholastic Ltd, 2013

ISBN 978 1407 13850 3

Printed and bound by L.E.G.O., Italy

2 4 6 8 10 9 7 5 3 1

Papers used by Scholastic Children's Books are made from woods
grown in sustainable forests.

A long time ago in a galaxy far, far away ...
It was a period of civil war and the Galactic Empire threatened to crush the Rebellion with its ultimate weapon, the Death Star ...

... until it was blown up.

With the Death Star destroyed, Princess Leia and the Rebel Alliance scored a major victory, but there was no time to celebrate.

Princess Leia announced, "Fellow Rebels, the Empire will surely hunt us down. So we must evacuate to our secret base on Hoth."

Then Princess Leia turned to her trusted allies Luke Skywalker and Han Solo.

"Luke," said Leia, "we fear an Imperial counter-attack may come from Naboo. I need you to go there and locate the stormtrooper base, then Han and I will lead the Gungan troops in to destroy it."

"Hey, you can count on me, sister," said Han.

"Me, too, sister!" Luke agreed awkwardly. "*Hmmm*, did that sound weird to you guys?"

"*Ewww*, yeah," said Leia to Han. "Kinda creepy."

As the Rebels blasted off to their missions, the sound of a toilet flushing filled the empty room. A golden droid walked out of the bathroom, looking confused.

"Um, hello, anyone?" C-3PO called out in despair. "They've left me. I'm all alone!"

*"Wahharrrghhh!"* yelled Chewbacca, who had also been left behind.

"I'm not alone!" C-3PO cried. "It appears that we are stuck here, but now we can be stuck here together!"

Having escaped the Death Star explosion, the evil Darth Vader glared at his generals on the Super Star Destroyer. "The Rebel scum who attacked us must be found and eliminated," he announced. "For your sake, Admiral, I pray you are up to the task."

"Yes, Lord Vader," answered the admiral nervously. "I've dispatched probe droids to hunt down Skywalker."

Darth Vader suddenly found himself surrounded by probe droids. He swatted them away.

NOT **THIS** SKYWALKER!

Back on Naboo, Leia and Han had flown in secretly to meet with Boss Nass, the leader of the Gungan army.

"Boss Nass," said Leia, "on behalf of the Rebel Alliance, thank you for your assistance with fighting the Empire."

"Wesa Gungan be happy to helpen yousa," exclaimed Boss Nass, who sent a tidal wave of drool all over Leia and Han as he talked. "*Biiiiig* happy to help!"

SAY IT, DON'T SPRAY IT!

While Han and Leia were drying off the Gungan slobber, the Emperor was making plans of his own.

"I have a brilliant plan to repay the Rebels for destroying the Death Star," cackled the Emperor.

"Bold thinking, my Master," said Darth Vader. "A lesser Emperor would have done something stupid like build *another* Death Star."

"Exactly!" the Emperor continued, not paying much attention to his apprentice. "I shall build another Death Star."

"Best idea ever," said Vader, quickly changing his tune.

"And the best part is," said the Emperor, "we can build it together … just me and my boys."

"Yes, Master. Wait – did you say *boys*?" asked Vader.

He turned around to see the Emperor's former apprentice, Darth Maul, acrobatically flipping, skipping, and bouncing towards them while slashing his awesome lightsaber through the air.

"Darth Maul is back!" declared the Emperor. "Isn't it wonderful?"

On the streets of Theed, Luke and R2-D2 stealthily followed a team of stormtroopers back to the Empire's base.

Luke ducked around a corner to call Leia and give her the news.

LEIA, IT'S LUKE. I'VE FOUND A BATTALION OF ...

GIRLS?

Luke's comlink conversation was suddenly cut short by a team of shrieking young girls!

"Oh my gosh, it's Luke Skywalker!" shouted one girl.

"You're famous!" said another, giggling.

"You blew up the Death Star!" exclaimed another. "And you're on my lunchbox!"

*"Shhhhh,"* whispered Luke. "Please, I'm on a secret mission."

"Secret mission!" shrieked all the girls at a piercing volume that drew the attention of the stormtroopers. The soldiers ran over to see what the screaming was all about.

"Hold it right there, Rebel!" said the stormtrooper.

FH-ZZMMMM

Swiftly, Luke launched into the air and caught his lightsaber, which R2 had shot to him from the ground. Wielding the lightsaber's plasma blade, Luke landed in front of the stormtroopers in an impressive battle stance.

"Wow, nice move!" cheered the stormtroopers, forgetting that they were supposed to capture the Jedi. "UH-OH!"

The stormtroopers tried to blast him, but Luke expertly parried their blasts and knocked them out.

"Oh, man," moaned Luke, suddenly regretting his cool move.

Instantly, the girls started screaming and chasing the young Skywalker.

"This is really not a good time for this," he shouted. Luke and R2 ran for their lives. "Please, leave me alone!"

The girls screamed in glee.

"Get him!"

"Can I have your autograph?"

As Luke sprinted through the unfamiliar streets of Theed, he decided to call for help. "Threepio, I need your help finding a way off this street. Threepio! Threepio!"

The protocol droid, who had just been fuming over being abandoned by his master, leaped into action. "Master Luke! Chewbacca and I are on our way to save you!"

With great strength, C-3PO grabbed Chewie, and yanked the Wookiee up the ramp and onboard the *Millennium Falcon*.

"No!" Luke hollered. "Don't come here! I just want ..." But it was too late. Help was on the way whether he wanted it or not.

Back on the Super Star Destroyer, the Emperor was trying to figure out the directions. "I'm gonna build a Death Star," he said. "Ohh … Boys, I really thought we could do this together."

But Darth Maul and Darth Vader had other ideas. They were having a lightsaber duel to deal with some Sithling rivalry.

"Stop that!" the Emperor shouted. He broke up the fight by shocking both Sith Lords with a steady stream of Force lightning. "Play nice!"

Just then one of the generals came with some good news. Luke Skywalker had been spotted on Naboo by one of the probe droids.

"I will go and personally crush him," proclaimed Darth Vader. "And then you'll see who's the most fearsome Sith Lord in the galaxy!"

Without C-3PO's guidance, Luke and R2 crashed through the crowded streets only to find themselves trapped in a dead-end alley. Frantically looking around for a place to hide, Luke discovered a costume shop! When the girls rushed down the alley, instead of finding Luke and R2, they discovered an odd-looking Darth Vader and an even weirder-looking Ewok.

OKAY, ARTOO. KEEP IT COOL.

NOTHING TO SEE HERE, JUST A SITH LORD OUT FOR A WALK.

But waiting around the next corner were more girls – hundreds of them. The word had got out, and the Jedi-ratzi were on the hunt.

"*EEEEEEEEE*, there he is!" the girls screamed. "We love the costume! You look good in black! We'll get you now!"

Luckily, Luke made it to the ship just in time and took off into space, barely escaping his mob of fans.

Luke sighed with relief, but soon realized that he still hadn't completed his mission. "Where am I going to get help?" he said, panicking. "Okay, calm down, Luke, calm down. Use the Force." Luke closed his eyes and concentrated on his next move.

Meanwhile, a TIE Fighter with the real Darth Vader in it was speeding straight towards Luke's X-wing, but the Sith Lord was too upset to notice. "I'll show that yellow-eyed bully!" he shouted. "Use the Force ... use the Force ..." Vader repeated, closing his eyes.

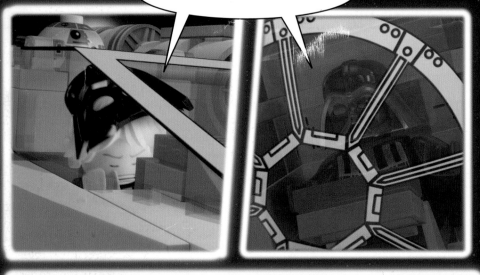

Suddenly, the two ships crashed into each other! The spaceships burst apart into many pieces, sending both pilots hurtling through space. Surprised and confused, Luke and Vader passed each other mid-flight before landing in the cockpits of their rebuilt ships and speeding off in different directions.

Tumbling out of control, Vader's TIE Fighter crash-landed in the dunes of Tatooine.

Vader shook his clenched fists into the air. "I have sand up my *nooooooose*! Other than that, I feel peachy."

Vader survived the wreck – just in time for a pack of Jawas to give him a stunning surprise.

ZAPP!

Luke wasn't faring much better. His ship veered off course and smashed through the control deck of an Imperial Star Destroyer. Opening his hatch to survey the damage, Luke staggered out of the X-wing, still dressed in his full Vader suit.

"Oh, my head hurts," he moaned. Luke soon noticed that he was surrounded by an Imperial army.

"Lord Vader, we are honored by your presence," said an Imperial general as the officers bowed down to Luke.

"Cool!" said Luke, realizing that the generals actually thought he was Darth Vader. Catching himself, he quickly switched to his best Vader impression. In a deep, husky voice, he said, "I mean, *cool.*"

Back on the *Millennium Falcon*, a nervous C-3PO fretted as Chewbacca piloted the ship through space.

"Step on it, Chewie!" commanded C-3PO. "We have to reach Naboo to save Master Luke. But first, look out for those asteroids!"

Chewie howled as they entered a crowded asteroid field and swerved in and out of the slow-moving massive space rocks.

While Chewie and C-3PO dodged asteroids, Han, Leia, and the Gungan fighters were waiting for the perfect moment to attack the stormtrooper barracks in Theed.

"These are Luke's last coordinates," confirmed Leia.

"And there's the secret barracks," Han added, stating the obvious and pointing toward the barracks surrounded by stormtroopers. "Now, what's crucial here is the element of surprise."

Out of nowhere, the *Millennium Falcon* crash-landed right on top of Han, Leia, and their Gungan companions. As C-3PO and Chewbacca fell out of the cockpit, the protocol droid proclaimed, "We have come to save you!"

Crawling out from underneath the crashed ship, Han and Leia noticed that a swarm of stormtroopers were rushing out of the barracks with their blasters aimed at the Rebel forces.

THAT'S JUST SWELL.

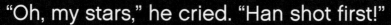

> OKAY, REBELS, HANDS UP. YOU ARE ALL UNDER ARREST.

Without warning, Han drew his blaster and fired at a stormtrooper, blowing him backwards. C-3PO was shocked.

"Oh, my stars," he cried. "Han shot first!"

"Of course I did, it was me or him," explained Han. "Why *wouldn't* I shoot first?"

"That is a subject of some debate," admitted C-3PO.

But the battle was not over yet. More stormtroopers opened fire on the Rebels as Chewie, Leia, and the Gungans joined in the fight.

SSSSSS

When Darth Vader came to, he was hanging upside down chained to a sandcrawler.

"How could this get any worse?" the Sith Lord asked himself.

Then a chittering Jawa began spray-painting Vader's jet-black helmet silver to make him look more like a droid.

Coughing from the fumes, Vader gasped, "Not the helmet! Oh! Right in the air vent."

Watto flittered over with a Jawa at his side and poked at Vader.

"You want me to buy this junk pile?" asked Watto. "No way!"

"Watto," exclaimed Vader. "My old master, it's me – Anakin Skywalker!"

"Right," said Watto with a chuckle. "And I'm Count Dooku. Crazy droid."

Finally, Darth Vader could not take any more embarrassment. He screamed.

Summoning all of his anger and strength, Vader ripped free of his chains and used the Force to transform the Jawas' sandcrawler into a playground. Then he hopped into Watto's podracer and zoomed off into the distance.

Deep in space, the new Death Star was slowly taking form. The Emperor, consulting his manual, used the Force to move bricks into place.

"My Death Star is coming to glorious life!" he cackled.

Suddenly, a hologram of the poorly painted Darth Vader appeared. "Master, I have found the Rebels and will soon eviscerate them!"

EXCELLENT!

The Emperor became puzzled. "Why do you look like you just crawled out of a junk pile?"

"No reason," said Vader, before his hologram quickly disappeared.

The Emperor turned to Darth Maul and gave him the instruction manual. "Keep working while I monitor the battle, okay?"

"You got it, Pops," laughed Darth Maul gleefully. "My turn ... and I think it needs more red bricks!"

Back at Theed, the battle between the Rebels and the Imperial forces continued. The remaining stormtroopers were quickly dwindling.

"I think that's the last of them!" declared Leia.

C-3PO began to celebrate, throwing his arms in the air and screaming, "In your face, Imperial scum!"

However, a new army of AT-ATs crushed forward and announced, "This is the Empire. Surrender, Rebels!"

LISTEN, I SAY, I HOPE I WASN'T OUT OF LINE WITH THAT BIT ABOUT 'IMPERIAL SCUM.'

Before the Imperial forces could annihilate the remaining Rebels, Luke Skywalker entered in his Vader suit, accompanied by several Imperial officers and R2-D2.

"I'll take it from here, General," said Luke Vader.

"Lord Vader," said the general, surprised. "You know, you're a lot shorter in person."

"And you're a lot dumber in person!" snapped back Luke Vader. "Now … I order you to destroy your barracks over there."

Although the order seemed ridiculous, one of the AT-ATs blasted the barracks, which erupted into a big explosion.

BOOM!

"That was neat!" said Luke Vader, breaking character. "Now, I'll just be leaving with these prisoners, and you—"

"Wait!" interrupted the real Darth Vader as he pointed to Luke. "This is an imposter!"

Using the Force, Vader unmasked Luke. The entire crowd gasped.

Luke drew his own lightsaber, preparing for battle. "Don't play nice with me, Vader. You killed my father!"

OH, REALLY? WELL, I'VE GOT SOME NEWS FOR YOU. NEWS THAT IS GOING TO BLOW YOUR MIND.

HERE IT COMES. RIGHT NOW. GET READY FOR A SPOILER ALERT.

LUKE, I AM YOUR FA—

Vader was just about to reveal a very impo{...} secret when he was interrupted...

"There he is!" squealed the team of girls that had been chasing Luke Skywalker. They quickly rushed up and mobbed Luke.

"Finally!" they screamed. "We knew we'd catch you!"

STOP IT!

I'M ABOUT TO ROCK HIS WORLD! LUKE, I AM YOUR—

Thinking quickly, C-3PO jumped in front of the girls and said, "You young ladies are mobbing the wrong chap." That got the girls' attention.

Then he pointed to Vader.

"Lord Vader is too modest to show you, but behind that evil mask you will find ... this!"

R2 swiftly p█████ed a photo of the young, dreamy Anakin Skywalker, which made the girls squeal with delight and turn their mobbing attention on the super-cute Sith Lord.

The girls chased Darth Vader. Once the villain and the crowd of teenage fans were gone, Luke turned to his friends and said, "Listen, I came here on a Star Destroyer that's ready to attack us."

"We need to take it down," said Leia. "Everyone to your ships!"

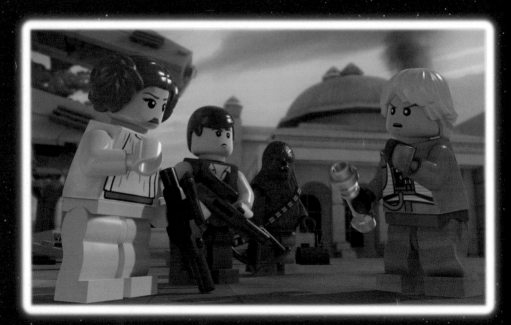

Just outside of Naboo, the Rebels found the Star Destroyer. "We'll never defeat Vader and his men," whimpered Luke.

"We will with Han on our side!" cheered Leia as the *Millennium Falcon* flew in to save the day once again.

But Han Solo wasn't flying the *Millennium Falcon*. C-3PO and Chewie were!

"Whoa! We're doomed! *Doomed!*" screamed C-3PO as their ship shook with the force of a giant explosion. The hit from enemy fire knocked C-3PO and Chewie down into the blaster turrets.

Hopelessly tangled up, the droid and Wookiee did their best to fire back at the swarming TIE fighters.

As the *Millennium Falcon* veered wildly through space, Luke's X-wing ducked in and around the larger Imperial Star Destroyer. Suddenly, Vader's TIE fighter zoomed back on the scene, zeroing in on Luke.

Darth Vader aimed his blasters at Luke's ship.

But just as it looked like Luke was a goner, a spaceship full of squealing girls rammed into Vader's ship.

*WHAT? OH, COME ON! GET A LIFE. DO YOUR PARENTS KNOW WHERE YOU ARE?*

Then, jumping into hyperspace, Vader tried to escape the swooning mob.

"Whoo-hoo! You're all clear, kid!" shouted Han Solo. "Now let's blow this thing and go home … again!"

With co-ordinated blasts from Leia, Luke, and Chewie, the Imperial Star Destroyer took a direct hit and exploded into millions of pieces.

"Blast! They got away again!" moaned the Emperor as he watched the end of the battle. "But I shall soon destroy them with my – ARGH! What is that?"

Instead of seeing the Death Star outside his window, the Emperor found a dreadfully ugly, gigantic image of Darth Maul's head.

HOW YOU LIKE IT, DADDIO? I TOTALLY AWESOME-IZED IT FOR YOU. NOW IT'S A **DARTH** STAR.

NO! NO! YOU SITH-HEAD! I CAN'T TERRORIZE THE GALAXY WITH THAT! I'LL BE THE LAUGHINGSTOCK OF THE EMPIRE.

Suddenly, Vader's TIE Fighter flashed out of hyperspace — followed closely by the girls in their spaceship — both on a collision course with the Darth Star. Before either ship could stop or slow down, they plowed into the newly built battle station, creating an enormous explosion.

"*Ooh*, we are so grounded!" cried the girls.

NOT MY BEST DAY.

Vader hurtled through space and a sea of bricks before crashing into the Emperor's Super Star Destroyer.

The Emperor crawled out from under the rubble and shouted, "Vader! Because of you, Darth Maul and my new Death Star are no more."

Vader braced himself for the worst punishment of his life...

But the Emperor just laughed and gave Vader a big bear hug.

That night, the Emperor held a celebration to name Darth Vader the "Evil Employee of the Month." And all was well in the Empire again.